MAKE IT RAIN

by Shanna Silva

All source images from Shutterstock.com

ISBN-13: 978-1-68021-156-6
eBook: 978-1-63078-492-8

Printed in Malaysia

22 21 20 19 18   1 2 3 4 5

Jackson Hill was not the best student. Most classes were hard for him. Computer class was different. He loved to write code, and he was good at it.

He started coding when he was 10. Computers just made sense to him. Sometimes they made more sense than people.

To earn money, Jackson built websites. Every dollar went to his mom. He wanted to help with the bills.

It was just the two of them. His dad had left years ago. Jackson didn't like to think about him.

His mom worked two jobs. She earned enough for their basic needs. But money was still **tight.**

One night, Ms. Hill got home late. Jackson was making dinner.

"Smells good," she said.

"Hi, Mom. Do you have to go back out?"

"Nope. You're stuck with me." She smiled.

"Good. We can watch *Make It Rain*."

Make It Rain was a game show. People tried to sell their ideas. The winner got a cash prize.

Jackson and his mom liked to watch it together. He had recorded it the night before.

After dinner, they sat on the couch. Jackson hit play on the remote.

Rico Moore smiled for the camera. He was the show's host. Jackson thought he was funny and cool.

Rico said hello to the guests. Then
it was time to hear their ideas.

Some were products. Others were services. There was also an app. That got Jackson's attention. He was working on one of his own.

But another idea stood out to him. A young woman invented a special bike helmet. It kept the head cool.

Many people could use it, she said. Members of bicycle clubs. Those who lived in hot places. It would be a hit. Jackson wished he had thought of it.

He picked the helmet to win. His mom liked to guess too. But she had fallen asleep.

Rico named the winner. It was the young woman. Jackson had guessed right! She won the money. The show owned the idea.

He got up to get a snack. Then he stopped. Rico was talking about a contest.

It was a special show for teens. Those with the best ideas would appear. The winner would get a big cash prize.

Casting events were set for major U.S. cities. One was in Atlanta. That is where Jackson lived.

"Mom! Wake up!" He hit rewind on the remote.

She sat up. "What is it?"

He pressed play. "You have to hear this."

His mom listened.

"Can I apply?" he asked.

"With what idea?"

"My **app.** Code Pro. It's perfect. Please, Mom!"

Ms. Hill sighed. She saw how badly he wanted this. But it might not work out. He would get his hopes up for nothing. It would be another letdown.

And there was her work. She would have to take time off without pay.

"I'll think about it," she said.

"Thanks, Mom." He knew better than to push.

The next morning, he went to the kitchen. His mom had left a note on the fridge. It said *Yes!* He pumped his fist in the air.

Jackson hurried to school. His best friend would not believe this. Mike liked *Make It Rain* too.

Jackson caught up to Mike. He told him about the show.

"I can't wait to see it," Mike said.

First, Jackson had to apply. The show needed to approve his idea.

He told his computer teacher about it. Mrs. Wiley was excited. She knew about his app. It was in the planning stage. This was a way to make it real.

She offered to help. After class, they went online. Together, they filled out the application.

A few weeks went by. There was no word from the show. Jackson was starting to worry.

He asked his mom about it. "What if they don't pick me?"

"Be patient," she said.

Another week went by. Jackson's phone buzzed.

"Any news?" Mike texted.

"Not yet," Jackson texted back.

"Too bad."

"Yeah, I know."

It was the next day. Jackson got home from school. Ms. Hill was waiting in the kitchen.

"This came in the mail." She handed him an envelope.

It was a letter from *Make It Rain*. He took a deep breath and opened it.

His eyes scanned the page. "I made it! I get to try out!"

Ms. Hill was relieved. "They know talent when they see it."

Make it Rain
3100 Century Park
Los Angeles, CA 94699

Jackson Hill
1010 Lake Blvd
Atlanta, GA 30314

The day of the tryouts came. They were held at a local hotel. Hundreds of teens showed up. Only three would be chosen.

It seemed like impossible odds. But Jackson wanted to stay positive.

He took his place in line. In his mind, he went over the app. He practiced what to say to the judges.

Finally, it was his turn. Jackson entered a room. Men and women sat behind a table. He stood and faced them.

For a second, he felt nervous. But then the questions started. Jackson relaxed. He felt confident as he spoke.

And then it was over. The finalists would get a call the next day.

He and his mom went home. That night, Jackson had a hard time sleeping. When he woke up, he checked his phone. He kept checking every few minutes.

Then the call came. His idea had been selected. He and his mom would fly to California.

Two weeks later, they landed in Los Angeles. A gift basket was waiting in their hotel room. The card was signed by Rico Moore. Jackson couldn't believe it. Rico was a big star.

Ms. Hill unpacked. But Jackson couldn't focus. His mind was on the show.

There was a real chance to win. His mom could quit her second job. The pressure was on.

It was the next morning. A limo came to the hotel. It took Jackson and his mom to the **studio**.

Ms. Hill sat in the audience. A woman led Jackson backstage. Two others were there.

Julie was from Texas. Her idea was a tool for styling hair. Todd from Utah had made a jacket. It closed with magnets instead of a zipper.

Rico Moore walked in. "Hi. I'm Rico."

"Wow!" Jackson said. "It's great to meet you!"

"Yeah, I know," Rico said. "You're the one with the app, right?"

Jackson nodded.

"That app is worth big bucks. It's a perfect setup," Rico said. He winked.

Setup? Jackson thought.

"Showtime," Rico said.

They took their places on the stage. "Go!" the director said.

After a few jokes, Rico turned to Julie. He asked about her styling tool. Jackson could tell she was nervous. She giggled the whole time.

Todd was next. His jacket with magnets was a good idea. But he looked down and spoke softly.

Then it was Jackson's turn. He looked into the camera and explained his app. But he kept thinking about what Rico had said. Something wasn't right.

At the break, he went over to his mom.

"Great job," she said.

"Thanks."

"Why aren't you smiling?" she asked. "You should be happy right now."

"I have a bad feeling."

"What do you mean?"

"This feels rigged," he said. "Like it's been decided. I'm going to win."

"Well, your idea is clearly the best."

The break was over. Everyone went back to their spots. It was time to name the winner.

"Jackson Hill!" Rico said. "You have the winning idea! Your app will make it rain."

Cheers came from the audience. Jackson looked over at his mom. She was cheering and waving.

He smiled at her. This is what he had wanted. But his stomach was in knots. Something was wrong. He needed answers.

Jackson went to Rico's dressing room. The door was partly open. Rico was wiping off his makeup.

Jackson knocked. "Can I talk to you?"

Rico looked over. "Sure, kid. Come in."

"You knew I would win. But how?"

"Does it matter?" Rico asked. "Take the money. Go home. Enjoy your life."

"What will happen to my app?"
Jackson asked.

"It's the show's app now. And it's
simple. People will download it. I'll
get rich."

Jackson frowned. None of this made sense. "The app is free," he said. "And you just said the show owns the app. How will you get rich?"

"Here's the deal," Rico said. "People put their info into the app. Then I sell it. It's easy money."

Jackson thought for a moment. Then it hit him. "Isn't that identity theft?"

"Call it what you want. There's big money in it."

"That's illegal. You can't use the app for that. I won't let you."

"Kid, I can do whatever I want. And don't bother telling anyone. I'm a star. Everyone loves me. No one would believe you anyway. You're nobody." Rico left the room.

Jackson was stunned. Rico was not cool at all. The guy was a creep and a criminal.

He found his mom and told her the story.

"You were right to **trust your feelings**," she said. "What he's doing is wrong."

"He won't get away with it," Jackson said. "I don't care if I lose the money."

"What are you going to do?" she asked.

He started texting. Then he hit send. "Remember when I told you the show felt rigged?"

She nodded.

"When I went to see Rico, my phone was recording the conversation. I just sent it to the bosses at *Make It Rain*. Now they will know what Rico is doing."

"You did the right thing, Son."

"It's not my app anymore. But I don't want it used to hurt people."

Jackson and his mom left Los
Angeles. They were glad to get
home.

Later that day, Jackson got a
call. It was an executive from
the show. She said that Rico had
been fired. There was more news
too.

"You were willing to risk your prize for the truth. We want to reward you. So we've doubled your winnings."

Then the story broke. It was all over the news. Social media was on fire. "Jackson Hill helps catch TV host criminal!"

Reporters waited outside his house. They all wanted interviews.

The excitement continued the next day at school. Jackson was a celebrity. Everyone wanted to talk to him.

He stopped by his computer class.
"Thanks for your help, Mrs. Wiley."

"I was happy to do it. Any big plans?"
she asked.

"Well, my mom quit her second job.
And I'm going to hire a tutor. I need
to get my grades up for college. I'm
going to study computer science."

"That's fantastic!" she said.

For the first time, Jackson was
excited about his future. Someday he
would make it rain for real.

TEEN EMERGENT READER LIBRARIES®
BOOSTERS

EMERGE [1]

9781680211542

9781680211139

9781680211528

9781680211153

9781680211559

9781680211122

9781680211146

9781680211337

9781680211573

ENGAGE [2]

9781680211290

9781680211535

9781680211313

The Literacy Revolution Continues with
New TERL Booster Titles! *Each Sold Individually*

EXCEL [3]

9781680214871

9781680211580

9781680214888

9781680211306

9781680211320

9781680214604

SOAR [4]

9781680211597

9781680211603

9781680211566

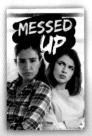
9781680214635

9781680214864

9781680214611

[TERL]

TEEN EMERGENT
READER LIBRARIES®

[1]
EMERGE

9781622508662

[2]
ENGAGE

9781622508679

[3]
EXCEL

9781622508686

[4]
SOAR

9781680213041

www.teenemergentreaders.com